AMY'S TRUE PRIZE

THE LITTLE WOMEN JOURNALS™
by Charlotte Emerson
from Avon Books

AMY'S TRUE PRIZE
BETH'S SNOW DANCER
JO'S TROUBLED HEART
MEG'S DEAREST WISH

Madame Alexander®

ALEXANDER DOLL COMPANY, INC.

The Little Women Journals™

—— AMY'S TRUE PRIZE ——

Charlotte Emerson

Illustrations by Kevin Wasden

AVON BOOKS NEW YORK

AVON BOOKS
A division of
The Hearst Corporation
1350 Avenue of the Americas
New York, New York 10019

Produced by By George Productions, Inc.
Interior illustrations copyright © 1998 by Avon Books
Interior illustrations by Kevin Wasden
Interior design by Kellan Peck
Visit our website at http://www.AvonBooks.com
ISBN: 0-380-97634-X

Library of Congress Cataloging in Publication Data:

Emerson, Charlotte.
    Amy's true prize / Charlotte Emerson.—1st ed.
        p.   cm.—(Little women journals)
Summary: Amy finds herself in a quandary when, after two of her paintings are accepted
for the Christmas festival artist contest, she discovers that one of her entries is actually a
work done by Marmee.
    [1. Honesty—Fiction. 2. Contests—Fiction. 3. Christmas—Fiction. 4. Sisters—Fic-
tion. 5. Family Life—New England—Fiction. 6. New England—Fiction.] I. Alcott, Lou-
isa May, 1832–1888. Little women. II. Title. III. Series: Emerson, Charlotte. Little
women journals.
PZ7.E5835Am   1997
[Fic]—dc21

97-7275
CIP

First Avon Books Printing: February 1998

Printed in the U.S.A.

FIRST EDITION

QPM   10   9   8   7   6   5   4   3   2   1

TABLE OF CONTENTS

Contents

AMY'S TRUE PRIZE

CHAPTER ONE

―――― ∞ ――――

But Little Amy . . .

"*A*my! Amy March! Jumping Jehoshaphat, where is the girl?" Jo March grumbled.

Amy curled herself into a ball on the sofa. She was surrounded by cushions, covered by a quilt, and cozy as could be. Why was it that just when a body got comfortable, somebody else—usually an older sister—had to come along and spoil it?

Of course, she *had* promised Jo that she would straighten up the dining room. And she planned to, any minute now. She had actually been heading there with her dust rag when she noticed her journal lying on the sofa. Then she'd found the end of a pencil in her apron pocket. Before she knew it, she'd burrowed into the pillows and was in the middle of a sketch of a round, gray-haired woman balancing presents in her hands while her shawl got tangled in her feet and two tiny kittens swatted at the fringe. It was far more fun to sketch than dust. Even Jo would have to admit that!

Amy giggled as she drew a round O for the woman's mouth. The sketch was a perfect likeness of her Aunt Carrol the way she'd looked when she arrived at the March home earlier that day.

Right now Aunt Carrol was having tea with Marmee in the snug "morning parlor" Marmee used for callers on days like this one, when it was cold and gloomy outside. Marmee was leaving for Boston that very afternoon, and Aunt Carrol had come by with presents for their Boston relatives.

Amy sighed. She didn't know how she'd get along without Marmee! Her mother was to spend three entire weeks—perhaps a month—at the home of her first cousin's daughter, Ella. Ella had only just had a baby, and was doing poorly. Marmee had offered to nurse her and take care of the baby until a servant could be hired. No one could nurture better than

Marmee—which was why Amy would miss her so much! She was eleven, and almost grown up, but she still needed Marmee.

In a short while their wealthy neighbor, Mr. Laurence, would be sending his carriage to take Marmee all the way to Boston. The house had been bustling all morning long in preparation. Marmee's trunk and parcels were packed and standing in the hall.

Amy had done her share of folding and fetching, making sure that Marmee's garments would arrive clean and pressed and that she would have everything she needed. Although she would miss her mother dreadfully, it was a comfort to know that Marmee would have plenty of clean handkerchiefs and two extra pairs of gloves in her glove box.

At that moment Amy thought she heard her name again. And this time, it wasn't Jo calling for her. It had been Aunt Carrol talking to Marmee. Were they discussing her?

Amy sprang up from the sofa and tiptoed to the door. She pressed her ear against it, but the wood was too thick. Only a few muffled words came through the door. Highly unsatisfactory! For what drama could one make of *scone* and *Ella* and *mittens?*

Just then, Amy heard quick footsteps heading down the hall. She bounded back from the door, jumped over the back of the sofa, and threw the quilt over her.

She heard the door open. "Amy?" Jo whispered.

Amy stayed perfectly still. She knew she shouldn't risk Jo's displeasure, but she wanted just a few minutes to herself to finish her sketch. It would be such fun to show it to Marmee before she left! She would laugh, Amy knew, at the reminder of kittens, confusion, and Aunt Carrol saying "MY, oh, my" at least seventeen times.

Amy longed to make her mother laugh, particularly since this past week, Marmee had been "very disappointed" in her behavior. Amy had borrowed Meg's cameo pin to wear to school without asking. That had been wrong, Amy knew. But Meg had left early for her job as a governess, and Amy just couldn't resist. She knew that Meg would generously lend her anything she had. Amy just had to wear the pin that very day!

It had looked so pretty on her pink and white dress. How was she to know that Meg had put it aside to get the clasp fixed? It had been the worst kind of luck when the pin had fallen off, and Amy had lost it.

Amy had dissolved into buckets of tears. She'd begged Meg's forgiveness. It had been a stormy af-

4

ternoon in the March household. Jo had shaken her head, and even sweet Beth had looked reproachful. Marmee had spoken sharply to her about taking things without asking permission.

Though Amy knew she had been wrong, she couldn't help thinking that she wouldn't have been in quite as much trouble if Meg had other pretty jewelry to wear. Oh, if only there were enough money to buy cameo pins for all the girls! And silk dresses, and bracelets that jangled every time one moved one's wrist. Amy thought that it must be perfectly dreadful to be fifteen or sixteen, like Jo or Meg, and have to wear the same party dress over and over again.

But the March family was not wealthy, and there was no money for extras. "We are rich in all things that matter," Marmee often said. It was true that their home was full of laughter and love, Amy had to concede. But would the addition of a garnet ring and a matching bracelet be so much more to bear?

It was wicked of her to complain, especially when Father was off serving as a chaplain in the war. Everyone was making sacrifices. Amy didn't mind making sacrifices, but it was ever so much nicer to make them while wearing a new blue silk taffeta dress!

Amy turned to a blank page in her journal.

Someday, I shall have a dozen pins, and a garnet ring. Someday when I am older, and marry someone very rich.

It's too Terible and Distresing to be only eleven years old! Especially when you are the baby of the family. And it is Most Terible of all to have a nose that is so flat. It refuses to be pointy and classical, no matter how I pull at the tip!

Amy drew a picture of a perfect Grecian nose. She wrote *Perfect Nose* next to it. Then, with a sigh, she turned back to her drawing.

But just then she heard the sound of her name again. This time she was sure of it. Peeking over the back of the sofa, she saw that Jo had left the door open a crack. Aunt Carrol was talking about her again! Amy hoped that Marmee hadn't told her the story of the cameo.

Amy hurried over to the crack in the door. She strained to listen as she took a dust rag out of her apron pocket. She could claim she was dusting if anyone caught her eavesdropping.

"All the girls in Ella's family have married so well,"

Aunt Carrol was saying. "I only wish the same could happen to your girls."

"It's too soon to talk of such things, Aunt," Marmee said. Amy knew that note in her mother's voice. Underneath the sweetness, she was really saying, *"This subject is now closed."*

"The girls are still quite young," Marmee went on. "And I will be satisfied if they grow up to be valued for their strong characters and good hearts."

Amy crouched down and pressed her ear against the crack. She closed her eyes, for everyone knew that one can hear better when one's eyes are closed.

"So you say," Aunt Carrol sniffed. "But you know perfectly well that if they don't marry, you and your husband won't be able to support them. Now, Margaret will have no trouble," Aunt Carrol went on, even though Marmee had begun to speak. "She has that fresh beauty which attracts suitors. Jo—"

Aunt Carrol paused. Unpredictable, merry Jo was hard to sum up, Amy had to admit. "Well, let us pray that her manner may smooth out as she grows more mature, for she's just fifteen. And certainly, I'll never deny that she has a generous heart."

"And a fine mind," Marmee interjected.

"Yes, I suppose," Aunt Carrol said. Amy knew that her great aunt didn't care much for intellectual accomplishments when it came to girls. "*Oh, pay no mind to Aunt Carrol!*" Jo had said once in a burst of exasperation. "*She can be a dear, but she is consumed with good society and right manners. I once saw her dote so over a young woman's lace-trimmed gloves. The gloves were quite lovely, but Aunt Carrol failed to see that the girl was in the deepest despair, crying floods of tears!*"

Jo could always sum up a character in such a way that made her sisters laugh, thought Amy. It was a pity that Aunt Carrol could not appreciate Jo's fine sense of humor.

"Still, if Josephine tames her tongue she could shine in a drawing room," Aunt Carrol mused. "And dear Beth plays so beautifully! She is such a sweet thing that I have no worries on that score. But little Amy—"

Amy pressed closer to the door. She held her breath.

But Marmee interrupted a bit sharply. "Aunt, really. Beth is a child, as is Amy! I think this conversation extremely premature."

"Beth is thirteen, dear, and it's never too early. You are forming their characters and accomplishments. You must pay mind to what fruits those accomplishments will bear."

Amy barely listened to Marmee's clipped suggestion that Aunt Carrol try the pear preserves. *What about me?* she wondered. *Why did Aunt Carrol say "But little Amy . . ." like that?*

"No thank you. I can't take preserves—bad for my digestion," Aunt Carrol fussed. "Amy, now. The other girls have their points, but it remains to be seen how Amy will turn out. All signs point to her being a beauty, but you never can be sure. She's only eleven. What she needs is an accomplishment. Something to make her stand out from the pack, you know."

"My, look at the time," Marmee broke in smoothly. "Aunt Carrol, it is too kind of you to concern yourself so with the girls. But we must let them grow up, and each find her own way."

"No, it is *you* that must—"

"Now, I really must go, or I shall be late when the carriage calls," Marmee interrupted firmly. "I don't like to abuse Mr. Laurence's generosity."

Amy looked at the clock on the mantel. The carriage wasn't to call for a good half hour yet, and Marmee had only to kiss the girls goodbye and put on her bonnet. There was plenty of time. But why waste it with nosy Aunt Carrol? Even Marmee would tell a good thumping fib if she had to.

Amy heard the sound of a chair scraping back.

Quickly, she dashed back to the sofa and jumped in among the pillows again. She opened her journal and took up her pencil, intending to finish her sketch. But her thoughts wandered as Aunt Carrol's words haunted her.

"It remains to be seen how Amy will turn out. . . .What she needs is an accomplishment."

It is sadly true, Amy wrote in her journal. I've not done very well in school this term. Jo says my spelling is atroshus. Atroshious. Oh, bother!

Amy chewed on her pencil. When Marmee had found out that she'd borrowed Meg's cameo, she had called her conduct disgraceful. And now Aunt Carrol had practically said that Amy wasn't worthy of being a March!

I may not do well in school, but Jo says it's only because I don't try. And I daydream. And I sketch things in my books instead of reading them.

Amy gazed down at her drawing. Why, sketching! That was something she was good at! Why hadn't Marmee told Aunt Carrol that? It was so unfair! Amy would have liked to march right in and show Aunt Carrol the drawing. But, most likely, reminding her aunt of how she'd almost tumbled down the porch stairs wouldn't win Amy any favor in Aunt Carrol's eyes.

The parlor door creaked and Jo poked her head in. She had a scarf tied around her hair and a dust cloth in her hand. It was too late for Amy to dive under the quilt again. She shrank back against the pillows. Jo could scold better than anyone in the house.

Amy heard Jo's skirts swish as she approached. Jo reached down, swiped at Amy's boot, then tickled her chin with the edge of the dust cloth.

"Hmmmm, I don't see a soul in the parlor," Jo murmured. "Empty, for once. That's because my sister Amy said she'd gladly help me with the housework, so she must be doing so. She must be flying about like an elf! Such a good girl!"

Amy giggled. Jo wasn't angry with her, only a bit exasperated. She put her journal aside and jumped up. "I'm just on my way, Jo. See? I have my dust cloth."

"Well, tally ho, you little good-for-nothing," Jo grumbled good-naturedly. "We want Marmee to leave with the memory of a clean and shining house, don't we?"

"Yes, Jo," Amy said meekly. She hurried off through the double doors to the dining room.

She knew that Jo had been teasing. But her words stung.

Good-for-nothing!

Amy sighed as she dusted a candlestick. It was bad enough being the youngest. But now she realized that her position in the family was worse than ever. She was in grave danger of being a positive disgrace!

CHAPTER TWO

Such an Accomplished Young Lady

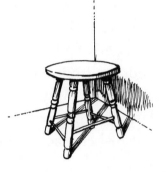

"*M*iss March!" Mr. Davis's face swam into Amy's view. The classroom, with its rows of desks, was silent as she descended from her daydream with a bump.

Oh, bother! Amy thought in despair. *I made so many resolutions to be good today!*

Amy had resolved that very morning to do better in school. She'd show Aunt Carrol and her family how accomplished she could be! She'd do her French lessons. She'd do her sums. And she would master spelling—even if it killed her.

But that thought had sent her off into a daydream. What would her funeral be like? Who would attend?

Amy pictured pots and pots of flowers, weeping ladies, and sad Concord gentlemen who would say, "I used to see the gay little thing about. If only she had clung to life just a bit longer! I would have waited for her and married her, if she would have had me. Her golden curls and her many accomplishments distinguished her from all others!"

Lost in her daydreams, Amy had not heard Mr. Davis call the class to order or begin the morning lesson. So the sight of her teacher looming over her was something of a shock.

"I'm so sorry to interrupt such *deep* thoughts," Mr. Davis said. "But would you mind handing me your lesson for today, Miss March?"

Amy blinked. "My lesson?"

"Yes, one usually brings one's lessons to school," Mr. Davis replied witheringly.

Oh, bother! She had left it at home! She knew just where it was, too. On her bedside table, next to her journal and pencils.

"Such hesitation tells me something, Miss March,"

Mr. Davis went on with a triumphant smile, for he dearly loved to catch students in the wrong. "It tells me that you did not do your lesson—"

"But I did, indeed, sir," Amy interrupted. "I just didn't bring it to school."

Mr. Davis's face was bright red. "Do not interrupt the teacher!" he thundered.

Amy shrank back against her seat. Mr. Davis could be so terrifying when he was riled! There wasn't a sound in the class. Each girl was afraid that if she made a sound, Mr. Davis would turn on her, too. It had happened before.

"Perhaps I would have overlooked your missing lesson," Mr. Davis continued, his face still very red. "But I do—not—overlook—interruptions, Miss March!" The clipped words rolled out like a rumble of thunder. Mr. Davis pointed his long, yellow finger at Amy.

"Sit in the corner, Miss March!"

The corner!

She would have to sit on a low stool, facing the class, for as long as Mr. Davis felt her infraction deserved.

Her cheeks scarlet, Amy rose and slipped past Mr. Davis. She sat herself on the hard little stool and faced the class, determined not to cry.

All the girls bent over their books again. No one

met her gaze. Amy's eyes filled with tears. She desperately cast about for something to think about: something gay, something amusing, something that would stop her tears as surely as a bucket of ice cold water.

I'll imagine I'm older, and going off to Paris. she thought. *What would I pack in my trunk?*

Amy started with one white ball gown for warm evenings. She pictured the gloves she would need, and hesitated over a blue cape or a rose-colored one. She conjured up images of tulle dresses and velvet cloaks, seventeen pair of gloves, and blue silk boots with French heels. She was just deciding whether she truly needed nine bonnets when Mr. Davis rang the bell and called for recess.

Happily, Amy stood and stretched her cramped legs. It would feel so good to dash about the school yard!

"Miss March, I did not give you permission to rise," Mr. Davis said sternly. "Sit down, miss. There will be no recess for you."

Amy sat. She felt hot tears gather in her throat again, for she considered further punishment horribly unfair.

Before her eyes, her classmates streamed from the room. Some, like her chum Kitty Bryant, gave her sympathetic glances. But May Chester and Jenny Snow dawdled as they walked by, and May Chester said:

"Such a pity Amy March hasn't learned manners! She's growing up quite wild. It's a positive disgrace, Mother says."

Anger coursed through Amy, and she contemplated a kick to May's passing form. It would be difficult to miss, for May was quite plump. But a moment later, self-pity swept over her instead, and tears spilled down her cheeks at last.

She *was* a disgrace, and all of Concord knew it!

Amy sat through recess in her corner. But as the students filed back in, Mr. Davis nodded at her, and Amy slipped gratefully back into her seat.

Determined to be a perfect student for the remainder of the day, Amy forced herself to pay attention. She focused on the tufts of hair that curled over Mr. Davis's upper lip. She willed her mind to concentrate and not think of elegant jewelry, sad funerals, happier days, and May Chester's nasty remarks.

The day crawled by. But at last Mr. Davis closed his lesson book. He cleared his throat, and the children in the class composed themselves to wait for the bad news regarding tomorrow's lesson.

"Class, before we talk about the lesson for tomorrow, I have an announcement," Mr. Davis said. "As you all are aware, the Concord Winter Fair is scheduled to open in a week's time at the Exhibition Hall. I have been asked to announce that there will be an art contest open to all the young people of Concord. If your work is selected, it will be in the exhibition at the Hall. There will be a grand blue ribbon award for the winner, and I believe the prize will be . . ." Mr. Davis looked through his spectacles at a piece of paper in his hand, ". . . a cash award, as well as an easel. The second prize will be a box of fine paints. And the third—the yellow ribbon award— will be drawing pencils."

A stir went through the class. Amy kept her gaze fixed on Mr. Davis. She knew everyone was looking at her.

Mr. Davis looked over his spectacles at the class. "Anyone interested should bring up to three samples of her artwork—just three, mind you—to Mrs. Lillipenny at the Exhibition Hall this afternoon until six o'clock, or tomorrow at the same time. I would encourage any artist to enter."

Behind her, Amy heard Ivy Bamford whisper,

"Why should we bother, since Amy March will win the blue ribbon?"

"Now," Mr. Davis said gravely, "as for tomorrow's lesson . . ."

Amy bent over her slate as Mr. Davis told them which sums to do and which pages to read in their books. She didn't hear a word of it.

At last, here was a way to redeem herself! Here was a way to show everyone that Amy March had a talent. She would choose her finest paintings. She knew she was the best artist in her class. Why shouldn't she be best in the city?

A cash prize could buy her so many pretty things! She had just seen a tiny garnet ring in a shop that was so much prettier than May Chester's little amber ring that she was so proud of. Amy imagined the deep red stone sparkling on her finger.

Then she remembered Meg's cameo, and she smiled. She could replace it! Perhaps there would be enough money to buy the ring and another cameo pin for Meg. Of course, the cameo might have to be smaller than the original had been, but Meg was so modest. A smaller pin might suit her even better.

Amy slipped into another daydream. She imagined a blue ribbon hung on her best work. Mrs.

Lillipenny would hand her the money. Amy would stand by the easel while all of Concord applauded.

Meg, Jo, Beth, and Marmee would be there. And Aunt Carrol! Amy smiled, picturing Aunt Carrol saying, "That Amy—such an accomplished young lady!"

Such an accomplished young lady!

"That ends our lesson for today. I will see you all *promptly* tomorrow," Mr. Davis finished.

Chairs scraped as the young ladies stood. They lined up politely to retrieve their cloaks and bonnets. Then they walked primly out of class. But as soon as they were outside in the fresh, cold air, conversation buzzed about the contest.

Kitty Bryant walked alongside Amy, her untied bonnet strings flapping. Kitty was her best friend and the sweetest girl she knew, but she could never manage to keep herself buttoned and tied.

"I know you'll win," Kitty told her. "You're so talented, Amy."

"I'm sure you shall, too," Mary Kingsley added, tucking in a wayward red curl.

"You're the best artist in the school," Katy Brown confirmed.

"I wouldn't be so certain about Amy winning."

Jenny Snow's cool voice floated toward them. She stood with May Chester, and the two girls smiled in a superior way at Amy, as though they knew something she didn't. The Snows and the Chesters were among the first families of Concord, and Jenny and May never forgot it for a moment.

Amy tossed her curls. "I'm not certain," she told them. "But we're all allowed to try, aren't we?"

"I'm just warning you to pick your very *best* drawings," May returned, smoothing down the fur around her neck. "There's a new girl who just moved to town named Adelaide Montgomery. Her father is a famous portrait painter in New York. Word has it that Adelaide has inherited his great talent."

"So you needn't be so high and mighty, Amy March," Jenny Snow flung at her. "When Adelaide enters the contest, you'll no longer be the best artist in Concord!"

CHAPTER THREE

The New Girl

*A*my hurried into the house. For a moment she had been excited, thinking what fun it would be to tell Marmee about the contest. But then she remembered that Marmee wasn't there. Amy sighed as she hung up her bonnet. She remembered Marmee's delighted laughter when Amy had given her the sketch of Aunt Carrol, just before Marmee left. Marmee had hugged her and whispered, "How shall I do without my Amy to cheer me during these gray November days?"

Not having Marmee to tell her news to was shockingly disappointing. But her sisters would be interested and ask her all sorts of questions.

"There you are at last, Amy," Jo said as Amy came into the parlor. Jo was sewing away furiously at a tear in the tea cloth. "How was your day? I need the hearth swept as quick as you please. Beth is busy in the kitchen, and I don't like to ask her."

"But I only just got home," Amy protested. "I want to go through my paintings, Jo, because—"

Jo looked up, exasperated. "Didn't you promise Marmee to mind me?"

"Yes, Jo," Amy said. She reached for the hearth broom. She decided then and there that Jo did not deserve to hear her grand news first.

"Now, let's have a chat while you sweep and I sew," Jo said in a kinder tone. "I never realized that there were quite so many confounded details to manage in order to keep this home running along like a well-wound clock. Marmee makes it all look so easy. Tell me about your day, Amy. It must have been better than mine. Aunt March had caller after caller today. I believe I made at least twenty-two pots of tea."

Jo made a comical face over her needle at Amy. She worked as a companion to Aunt March. Although Jo could coax a smile from the crotchety old woman better than any of them, her duties were sometimes tedious. "How I long for adventure!" Jo often said.

"Now, 'fess. Tell me about school," Jo said.

Amy decided to leave out her session in the corner of the schoolroom. There was no need to tell her sisters that she'd disgraced herself once again.

"Mr. Davis made an announcement at the end of school today," she said excitedly. "The Winter Fair is coming up, and there's to be a contest for young artists, and I—"

"Oh, drat!" Jo sucked on her finger. "Why is it that the needle seems to poke right through just where it shouldn't? What was that, dear?"

"Amy!" Meg rustled into the room, a frown on her pretty face. "You're here at last. How was your day? You must help me get the tea things. Miss Crocker said she might drop in, for she promised to keep an eye on us while Marmee is away."

"Not that old busybody," Jo grumbled.

"It can't be helped, so let's not fuss about it," Meg said, hurrying back toward the kitchen. "Hurry and finish, Amy. Do you think we need to use the good china? Oh, I do hope we have sugar!" she called over her shoulder.

Amy had made her most solemn promise to her mother that she would be good and cheerful while Marmee was away. But her sisters were trying her patience dreadfully.

Even her dear Meg was acting so terribly bossy! She could not get in a word to tell them about the fair.

And then there were the tea things to fetch, and the mended cloth to be spread on the table. And then Meg insisted that the room needed a quick dusting. The sisters flew about, arranging, patting, and smoothing, while Beth mixed up a ginger cake in the kitchen.

Amy's steps dragged. She was anxious to run upstairs to her room to go through her sketches and drawings. But every time she seemed to have a minute, Jo or Meg had another task for her. Amy moved more and more slowly, hoping that Meg would see that she was tired and send her upstairs. But it just made her fall further behind.

By the time tea was over and Miss Crocker went out the door with many insincere wishes to "call again soon," Amy had run out of patience. When Meg asked her to help Beth with the dishes, she burst into tears.

Jo frowned and was about to say a cross word,

but Meg gave her a warning look. Sixteen-year-old Meg considered Amy her special pet, and she put an arm around her and drew her close.

"What is it, dearest?" Meg asked in a soothing tone. "We've been running you ragged, I daresay."

"It's just that I have such news, and nobody cares," Amy sobbed.

"Of course we care, dear," Beth said tenderly.

"Tell us," Jo urged. "We're frightful, but we do want to hear, Amy."

Feeling a bit better, Amy dabbed at her tears with her handkerchief while she told her news of the Winter Fair.

"And Mr. Davis announced that we must bring in our paintings today in order to qualify, and it's nearly six." Amy concluded with a sniff. Mr. Davis had said she could bring in her drawings tomorrow, but she did so want to enter first thing, and it was only a *small* fib.

"Jumping Jehoshaphat, why didn't you say so, Amy?" Jo burst out. "Of course you must enter. Let's all pitch in girls, and help Amy get her bundle together."

"You still have time," Meg said, giving her an affectionate squeeze.

"I can do the tea things myself in a twinkling,"

Beth said, her soft eyes shining at Amy. "Oh, I'm sure you'll win, Amy. Your paintings are so fine!"

"Come on, Meg, let's help the girl, there's a good sport," Jo said cheerfully. "Poor little thing, I ran over her today like a runaway train. Though I do think it's all that old Croaker's fault. She puts us in such a tizzy!"

"You promised Marmee not to call Miss Crocker that name," Meg said primly to Jo.

"Oh, bless me, I did," Jo said with a sigh. "What a shame, when it suits her so well. She sniffs, and looks down her nose at us, and peers into our faces in order to ferret out our faults. Well, come on, Amy, let's go bundle up some masterpieces. Meg will wrap them in brown paper for you. Hurry, now."

Gratified by her sisters' interest, Amy hurried upstairs with Jo and Meg. She spread out her drawings, and Meg and Jo argued good-naturedly about which was best.

"I can only submit three," Amy said finally. "So we must choose."

"I say the painting of the river," Jo said decidedly. "Look at that lovely green, and the way she captured the sunlight on the water."

"But the autumn scene is such a blaze of red and orange," Meg said. "And I adore this sketch of Beth's dolls, too. Perhaps she should submit a landscape and a portrait."

"What are these, Amy?" Jo asked, pulling out a pad with a number of watercolors.

"Oh, I forgot about those," Amy said, hurrying over to examine them. "They are from when Marmee and I went out sketching last spring."

"These are capital," Jo said. "Take this one, Amy, of the weeping willow by the river. I like the little red boat in the corner, there."

"Yes," Meg agreed. "It's one of your best. Don't you agree, Amy?"

"Yes," said Amy. "I think it's the perfect choice."

"If we choose that, we should choose the autumn scene as well," Meg said in a decided tone. "Now, what should we choose for the third?"

"The dolls," Jo said. "You're right, Meg. Look at those faces. Amy has captured them perfectly. They look so sad and sweet, somehow."

Amy leafed through the drawings. Some of Marmee's delicate plant studies were mixed in with her own work, and she pushed them aside.

"Meg! Jo!" Beth's anxious voice called from downstairs. "Can someone come down, please? I burned my hand, and the soup pot is boiling over, and the kittens are getting under my feet—"

"Be right there, Bethy!" Jo called. "I'll go," she said to Meg.

"No, I'll go," Meg said, starting for the door. "You'll probably drop one of the kittens in the soup pot. You help Amy."

"But I'm such a wooly-fingered girl when it comes to wrapping up things nicely," Jo said, gathering the drawings and looking for brown paper at the same time.

"I'll be right back, then," Meg called from the hallway.

"Oh, do hurry, Jo," Amy said.

"I will, if you find me some string," Jo said, distractedly trying to fold brown paper with one hand and holding the drawings aloft with the other.

Amy ran for the string. But Beth had used it to wrap Marmee's packages for the trip, and had forgotten to put it back in Marmee's basket. Amy had to hunt for it in Beth's room. Then she couldn't find the scissors, and had to run downstairs to her own workbasket. By the time she had returned, Jo had the paintings wrapped in brown paper.

"There," Jo said, winding the string around the bundle and cutting it. She tied a quick bow. "Now, you'd better run. It's nearly six."

Amy tucked the slim package under her arm and

hurried downstairs. Jo helped her find her bonnet and gloves, and within a moment she was running down the lane, kicking through the dead leaves and taking deep breaths of the cold evening air.

At the town square, the Exhibition Hall lamps were still lighted as Amy ran up. She wasn't too late, then!

Amy burst inside, searching for Mrs. Lillipenny. Around her, people were stringing banners and garlands. The sound of hammering filled the air as workmen built the booths that would line the walls of the grand hall.

Spotting Mrs. Lillipenny behind a desk in a corner, Amy hurried toward her. A girl she didn't know stood in front of the desk. She was dressed all in brown, and her dark hair was wound into a braid that coiled around her head.

"Now," Mrs. Lillipenny was saying to the girl as Amy drew closer, "Here is the receipt for your painting." She handed the girl a small white card. "You'll receive another card in the mail if your painting is chosen as an entry in the contest."

"Thank you," the girl murmured politely. She turned and caught sight of Amy. She nodded briefly, and Amy nodded back, trying not to stare curiously.

She'd only just then realized that this must be the "new girl," Adelaide Montgomery.

Amy only had time to note her large, light gray eyes. Above them, dark brows swooped like wings. Her eyes are her best feature, Amy decided, sneaking another peek. Her face was thin and pale. Aunt Carrol would certainly not call her a beauty.

Still, Jo would say she looks interesting, Amy thought as she handed Mrs. Lillipenny her package.

"Three paintings for the contest," Amy told her. She peered at Adelaide's package, hoping to catch a glimpse of her work, but the package was securely wrapped.

"Here you are, Amy," Mrs. Lillipenny said, handing her back a card. "This is your receipt. I've had so many entries this evening," she said with a smile. "I'm afraid you'll have some competition. You'll be hearing from the judging committee next week."

"Thank you, Mrs. Lillipenny," Amy said.

Just then her friend Kitty Bryant walked up behind her. "I don't think you have to worry about the other entries, Amy," she told her as she handed Mrs. Lillipenny her package. "You're going to win that blue ribbon."

Amy wished that Kitty hadn't spoken so loudly. Adelaide turned and looked at her curiously. Then again, Amy thought, she was glad that Kitty had spoken. After all, she was worried about competition from Adelaide. Why shouldn't Adelaide worry, too?

Kitty thanked Mrs. Lillipenny for her receipt. Then she turned to Amy. "Ivy and Mary are waiting on the steps. We can all walk home together, if you like."

"I'm ready," Amy told her. She hesitated a moment, wondering if she should ask the new girl to join them. Amy glanced over and caught Adelaide looking at them. Amy smiled, but Adelaide lifted her chin and quickly glanced away.

Amy flushed. What a snob! She linked arms with Kitty and walked by Adelaide without a glance. She tossed her blond curls, hoping that Adelaide would think that Amy March possessed too much grace and confidence to feel a snub.

A tall woman entered the hall. She was dressed in worn black clothes and a brown bonnet. Amy watched as she beckoned to Adelaide, and the girl hurried toward her.

If her father is so famous, why are their clothes so dull? Amy wondered. But perhaps the ways of artists were different from ordinary folk.

Well, if *she* ever became a famous artist, she wouldn't dress in shabby, drab clothes, Amy decided. *I shall be the talk of society,* Amy thought, dreaming of shimmering ball gowns, sparkling jewelry, and bonnets trimmed in lace.

On a cold, snowy Tuesday the following week, the sisters gathered around the fire in the gathering twilight. They were putting together a package of gifts as a surprise for Marmee. Beth was sewing a rag doll for Cousin Ella's baby. Amy had offered to make a smock and nightcap for the doll. Jo was hemming delicate linen handkerchiefs for Ella, "for I don't believe even I can ruin a handkerchief," Jo had said ruefully. Meg had decided to embroider a pair of slippers for their cousin. She was best of all the sisters at embroidery.

Amy looked up when she heard a noise from the porch. "Was that the postman?" she asked anxiously.

"I'll go," Jo said, springing up. "I'm just about cross-eyed from all this needlework."

Jo hurried into the hall. Amy's heart raced as she heard the sound of Jo checking the mailbox. She should be hearing from Mrs. Lillipenny any day now. The suspense was just too much to bear!

Jo hurried back into the parlor waving a package of letters.

"There's a letter from Marmee. But look—here's one for Miss Amy March!"

"Oh, you open it, Jo," Amy said. "I'm sure I'm much too *agitatated*."

"Just be glad you're not being judged on pronunciation," Jo said as she slit open the envelope. "My, I feel agitated myself." Jo scanned the letter. " 'Thank you for your entry in the Winter Fair Art Festival . . .' et cetera, et cetera. My, Mrs. Lillipenny is long-winded. . . ."

"Well?" Amy demanded. She jumped up in a fever of impatience. "Don't keep me waiting, Jo!"

"Two of your paintings have been accepted!" Jo cried, breaking into a smile. "It certainly took Mrs. Lillipenny long enough to get to the point. The news is in the third paragraph. Let us now bow our heads and be glad that Mrs. Lillipenny doesn't write for our newspaper."

"Hurrah!" Beth cried, tossing her pillow in the air.

"I knew you would be accepted," Meg said, giving Amy a hug.

"I wish Marmee were here!" Amy exclaimed. "I'm so excited!"

"The fair will open on Thursday and run through Sunday," Jo said, still reading. "Prizes will be awarded on Saturday evening. That's jolly! You can roam about on Sunday after you win, and soak up all the praise."

"Do you really think I'll win?" Amy asked.

"Of course you shall," Jo said stoutly.

"Your work is so lovely! Of course you'll do well," Meg said. "The important thing is to do your best, Marmee says, and not yearn for rewards."

Amy nodded. But inside, she was seething with excitement.

I'm sure Marmee is right, she thought. *But I still want first prize!*

CHAPTER FOUR

Opening Night

Will Thursday never come? Amy wrote in her journal the next afternoon. She sat curled in her favorite corner of the sofa. For once, Meg or Jo wasn't fussing at her to dust the bookcase or sweep the kitchen floor.

Meg, Jo, and Beth will attend the fair on Friday evening. But I could never wait so long. Kitty said her mother will take us on opening night. Oh, I can't wait!

My one consullashen is my new dress. At least I don't have to wear one of Cousin Florence's horrid frights to the fair. It's too groosome to be so poor! Wearing hand-me-downs is the very most beastly thing about it. Here is a picture of the dreadful gown I had to wear until Marmee made me a new one:

Here, Amy drew a picture of a plaid frock with a stiff ruffle around the neck. That ruffle never failed to scratch her chin. She had to get out her drawing pencils to do the "fright" justice. Carefully she colored in a sick greenish shade. She drew the lace like sharp needles sticking straight up in order to catch the tender flesh of the neck and chin of the wearer.

And it was a great deal more dreadful than that! she wrote scornfully in the margin.

But on Thursday evening, I shall stroll everso casualy . . . casually through the Exhibition Hall. I shall wear my pink dress, and I shall not act at all proud, either. Perhaps someone will say, "Who is that delite . . . delightful creeture in the pink gown?" And someone will answer, "That is Miss Amy March. Have you seen her painting? I've never seen such a talent, even in the great capitles of Europe!"

Amy dropped her pencil and hugged her knees. "I'll show them all—Jenny, and May, and Aunt Carrol. Oh, I can't wait!" she whispered.

On Thursday evening Mrs. Bryant struggled to keep up with Kitty and Amy. The two girls had begun their walk in a ladylike fashion, but as they drew closer to the Exhibition Hall, they began to skip with impatience.

"All right, then," Mrs. Bryant finally said with a laugh. "Run along ahead, and I'll find you—right about when you'll be wanting me to buy you a glass of cider, I suppose."

"Thank you, Mama," Kitty said. She slipped her hand into Amy's. "Come on, Amy!"

"Thank you, Mrs. Bryant." Amy was just able to finish the words before Kitty tugged her forward with a jerk.

With quickened steps, Amy and Kitty made their way toward the brightly lit hall. People were streaming up the stairs. They called to one another in high, excited voices. Amy felt a thrill of pleasure. She could not imagine how delightful it would be to win a prize at such a grand event!

As they drew closer, Amy could hear a band playing a lively polka.

"Isn't it grand?" she asked Kitty, squeezing her hand.

"It's positively thrilling," Kitty declared. "Oh, I wish I were old enough to dance!"

"I don't think there's dancing, just music," Amy said with an important air, though she was basing her answer on a vague memory of Marmee's description of last year's fair, which she hadn't attended. "But I'm sure that when we are old enough, you won't lack for partners," she added loyally.

Once inside the hall, Kitty and Amy were swept into a swirl of movement. Ladies and gentlemen promenaded down the wide aisles, looking at the pots of blooming plants and pretty bric-a-brac for sale. Delicate pastries were arranged on silver trays on one table, and Amy's mouth watered as she gazed at them.

"Look, there's Adelaide Montgomery," Kitty whispered.

Adelaide wore the same drab brown dress, but she held her chin high in a composed fashion Amy couldn't help but admire. Her dark brown hair gleamed under the lights, and a cool smile was on her lips as she surveyed the crowd. *She looks as though she's too good for everyone,* Amy decided.

"Would it be proper to introduce ourselves?" Kitty

whispered. "Oh, bother, I forgot to button my gloves. How does Adelaide manage to look so grand in that shabby dress? I long to meet her and ask her about her famous father."

While Kitty struggled to button her gloves, Amy hesitated. She didn't care to meet Adelaide. She had a feeling the girl would just smile at her in that superior way, and Amy would feel drab and poor. Not to mention that it was so much easier to compete with a person you didn't know.

"Let's see the exhibition first," Amy suggested. "That way, we can compliment her on her painting if we like it."

"Amy March!" Lucretia Spade, a fellow classmate, hurried up to them. "I saw your paintings," she said breathlessly. "They are very fine. I'm sure you'll win the blue ribbon. Your sketch is up, too, Kitty," she added politely.

"Where are they?" Kitty asked, craning her neck in an attempt to see above the crowd.

"That corner there," Lucretia said, pointing.

But there were too many people crowded around the exhibition to see much of anything. Amy and Kitty pressed forward. As they tried to move through the crowd, they bumped into a solid gentleman in front of them. He turned, and it was Mr.

Davis. What a disagreeable thing, to have to see your horrid schoolmaster outside of class!

But outside of the schoolroom, Mr. Davis didn't seem quite so threatening. He merely gave them an amiable smile and a bow.

"Good evening, young ladies. Miss March, I have been to see your charming paintings. Very good work, I must say. I certainly hope one of you girls take the grand prize. It would be very good for the school."

"Thank you, Mr. Davis," Amy said politely. If only she could stop hearing about her paintings and actually see them!

Mr. Davis gave them a stiff smile and moved off. Mary Kingsley and Ivy Bamford rushed up to them. Mary's bright red hair was tied up in a yellow silk ribbon, which gave her a festive air.

"Amy, your paintings are on the wall!" Mary exclaimed. "And your sketch, Kitty. Oh, Amy, I'm sure you'll win the grand prize!"

"Yours are the best of the show," Ivy told her, nodding. "I like the river landscape. It makes me feel so sleepy and quiet, somehow. Your paintings are much better than Adelaide's entry, Amy. You have nothing to fear."

"I'm partial to your *Hollyhocks in the Garden*," Mary said.

"Oh, yes, the hollyhocks will win, for certain," Ivy agreed, for she was not a girl who was staunch in her convictions.

Hollyhocks? Amy thought, puzzled. *I never painted hollyhocks. The girls must be mistaken.*

Even more anxious to see, Amy left the girls and weaved through the crowd. Finally, she burst through to the exhibition area.

Her river landscape was on the wall, looking remarkably fine, in Amy's opinion. And the name *Miss Amy March* looked so elegant written out in a fine script!

But Amy smothered a gasp when she saw the next painting on the wall. It was a fine painting of hollyhocks in a green, blooming garden. Next to the painting, the small white card read *Miss Amy March.*

There was only one problem. Amy hadn't painted it. Marmee had!

CHAPTER FIVE

A Dreadful Mistake

*P*anic shot through Amy. People pressed close around her, and she felt suddenly warm and dizzy. She saw Mrs. Lillipenny only a few paces away. She took a step toward her, then stopped.

"Amy! Amy dear!" Aunt Carrol sailed into view like a huge gray barge. She wore a gray cloak trimmed in white brocade, and a dove gray bonnet trimmed with white feathers. A feather waved as Aunt Carrol bobbed her head at Amy. "What a *surprise! What* a surprise! Of course, I'd heard you were handy with your drawing pencils, my dear, but I never expected such accomplishment! Such accomplishment! The hollyhocks! So charming! I am very impressed, young lady!"

Amy blinked at Aunt Carrol. She felt so queer and dizzy. She had already lived this scene in her daydreams. Only Aunt Carrol had been talking of *her* paintings—not Marmee's!

"Look at you, so modest!" Aunt Carrol burbled, patting her shoulder. "Excellent, excellent!"

Beaming another approving look at her, Aunt Carrol swept off. Amy stood for a moment, not knowing what to do. Someone pointed at her and said something to her companion, who looked at Amy, then at the hollyhocks. Then she looked back at Amy and smiled and nodded.

Oh, what was she going to do?

Amy gazed about in confusion. She groaned under her breath when she saw that Jenny Snow was making a beeline for her. It was too late to run.

"I suppose I should congratulate you," Jenny said as she came up, her taffeta dress rustling. "Everyone is saying that you shall win."

Amy felt as though she'd been turned to stone. She just gazed at Jenny.

"But I'm not so certain, myself," Jenny went on

with a sniff. Her green eyes flicked over Amy, most likely making disdainful note of the fact that Amy was wearing her school dress to the Fair.

"Amy!" Kitty hurried up to her. "Isn't it grand? The hollyhocks are so pretty! I'm sure you'll take first prize!"

"*Are* you?" Jenny Snow asked haughtily. "I do hope your confidence is not misplaced."

Amy turned to Kitty. "I must go," she blurted. "I . . . the heat . . . the people . . ."

"Are you feeling faint?" Kitty asked, concerned. She looked around. "I'll find Mama."

"No, don't bother her. I just need some . . . air," Amy said haltingly. "I'll be quite fine. Please thank her for me. Good night."

Amy said the last words in a rush. Then she turned and rushed away. All she wanted to do was to be swallowed up by the crowd.

But she was stopped time after time on the way to the door, as friends and neighbors congratulated her. They usually mentioned the hollyhocks.

It was exactly how she'd pictured it would be. Amy tried to say composed "thank you's" and "how kind of you to say."

But inside she was reeling. Praise which should

have been sweet was dreadful to bear. Whatever was she going to do?

"How was the fair?" Jo asked as soon as Amy slipped into the house. She had closed the door as quietly as she could, but her three sisters crowded into the hallway to greet her.

"How did your paintings look?" Meg asked eagerly.

"Which was your favorite?" Beth asked.

Amy took off her bonnet. She longed to confide in her sisters, but she wanted to think everything over first. If only Marmee were here! She needed her mother's calm reason and gentle ways more than ever.

"The fair was lovely, and my work looked fine, I think," Amy said, as Meg helped her out of her cloak.

She saw Jo exchange a puzzled look with Meg and Beth. Her sisters knew her too well. It was odd that she didn't sound more excited.

"But I've got a dreadful headache," she said quickly.

"It's all the excitement," Meg said.

Beth nodded, her expression changing to concern. "And the crowds."

"It's everything all together, I expect," Jo said. "And you hardly ate a bite of supper, Amy."

"Come, I'll help you to bed," Meg said. "What you need is a cool cloth on your forehead."

"You need peace and quiet," Beth advised.

"And no chores to do," Jo teased, but Amy could only summon up a weak smile.

Amy allowed Meg to lead her upstairs. She was quiet as Meg helped her into her nightgown and brushed her hair. She slipped into bed, and Meg put a cool cloth on her forehead.

"Any better, dear?" Meg asked softly.

"Much," Amy said, with a grateful smile. Meg was so good! She wished she could tell her what had happened. Perhaps tomorrow she would " 'fess," as the sisters called it.

As soon as Meg had closed the door, Amy reached for her journal.

Jo always tells me that I must learn to look at things with Logic. She says that when you're troubled about something, you need to examine it from all sides, so it will become clear.

So. Here I shall attempt to Organize my thoughts.

Amy pondered for a moment. Then she wrote at the top of the page THE RIGHT THING TO DO.

1. *Withdraw Marmee's painting. Because I didn't do it.*

But was it that simple?

2. *Not withdraw the painting, because it's Teribly Unfair that I should be punished just because Jo put the wrong painting in the package.*

Amy chewed on her pencil, thinking. Anyone would say that Marmee's painting was only a *bit* better than hers. If everyone thought that she could have painted it, well, then, surely she could have.

Now, *there* was a piece of logic even Jo couldn't dispute!

3. *So if I don't remove the painting, and I get the prize, I will almost deserve it.*

And no one will know, after all. Marmee is going to miss the fair, and none of my sisters will recognize the painting. Why, Jo packed the lot, and thought it was mine, most likely!

And I've planned to buy Meg such a grand present if I win. It's not as though I am a selfish, greedy person.

I know Pride is a Deadly Unpardonable Sin. But Marmee says that pride in one's accomplishments is natural. So doesn't that mean that if my pride is at stake, I should let everyone think the painting is mine???

Oh, dear, Alas! Why, oh, why is it so hard to be good?

Amy sighed deeply. Would it be so very wrong to say nothing?

It didn't *feel* wrong.

"Examine your heart with a fair and honest mind, and you can never go wrong," Marmee often said.

"Well, I'm being honest," Amy said to herself as she closed her journal and shut out the light. "It would be only fair if I won the prize. And it's too tempting when no one will know the difference!"

She drew up the covers and closed her eyes. She would say nothing, she decided uneasily. After all, no one would know, and she had already worked out in her head that it wouldn't be terribly wrong.

Of course, if she won, her conscience might trouble her, just a little bit.

But she would be able to face Jenny and May. She would win a graceful easel and enough money to buy Meg a pin. And everyone would praise her. So, most likely, she could bear up under the strain.

CHAPTER SIX

Jo Tells a Story

*T*he next day at school, the class was abuzz with talk about "Amy March's great success." Amy did not enjoy the praise as much as she'd imagined. Had she made the wrong decision after all?

She had passed an uneasy night, and this morning, she had been almost glad that Marmee was not facing her across the breakfast table. Marmee's honest eyes could be a trial for an uneasy conscience.

Even Mr. Davis singled her out for special praise, saying with a knowing glance that "Miss March could accomplish much, if she could keep herself off corner stools."

After school, Jenny Snow and May Chester came up to Amy as she waited for Kitty and Mary. May was wearing a new bonnet trimmed in lace that framed her round face. Amy noted sourly that May kept touching it, as if to make sure it was still there, continuing to impress all who gazed upon it.

"Did you see Adelaide's painting?" May asked her with a significant look at Jenny.

"No, I didn't see much of the exhibit," Amy admitted.

"Well, then," Jenny said, "that must be why you are so confident today. For if you had seen the painting, you wouldn't be so sure of your success. Adelaide is so accomplished!"

"I'm sure that she is," Amy replied steadily. "And it is not *me* who is saying I'll win the grand prize, but others. I can't help what others say."

"Still, it must be hard to adjust to *second place*," Jenny said, and May giggled.

The tip of Jenny's sharp nose was bright red from the cold. For a moment, Amy was tempted to ask if Jenny would like to borrow her chalk in order to powder it. But such a remark would be unkind. "*One should repay unkindness with kindness, no matter how difficult it may be,"* Marmee often said.

But Marmee hadn't gone to school with Jenny Snow!

"Amy isn't going to get second place!" Kitty cried, for she had overheard the comment. "She's going to win! And won't you two look foolish then!"

"Hush, Kitty," Amy told her. "It's all right."

"Yes, hush, Kitty," Jenny said. "I'd pay more attention to your stocking, which has fallen into your boot, and stop worrying about defending little Michelangelo."

May and Jenny laughed as Kitty glowered. Then they strolled off, still giggling.

"It's not all right," Kitty muttered, as she bent over to straighten her stocking and her bonnet fell off. She snatched it up and plopped it on her head. "They're jealous of you, Amy, because you have talent and heaps of friends, and they just have fine clothes and each other."

"Did you see Adelaide's painting?" Amy asked Kitty curiously.

"Yes, and it wasn't as good as yours," Kitty said staunchly. "Not nearly. Besides, it's only one, so you have double the chance with your river painting and those dear sweet hollyhocks. Oh, I can't wait for you to show up those two!"

It's my duty now to keep the painting in the show, Amy told herself as she marched home with Kitty at her side. *I can't let Kitty down. And Jenny and May would make me the laughingstock of the school if I withdrew it. Why, they'll say I sent in the painting as mine on purpose, or some such thing!*

No, Amy decided. *I can't go back now.*

That afternoon Amy went about her chores with cheerful good will. She swept the hearth, dusted the parlor, and set to finishing the rickrack on her doll smock with great determination.

"I wonder where Jo could be," Meg said as she poked at the fire. "She should have been home an hour ago. We have so many chores to do if we want to set off for the fair this evening. We're to have an early tea this afternoon, and then a light supper before we go. And we want to send Marmee's package off by the evening post."

"I hope Aunt March hasn't caught cold again," Beth said.

"Yes, that would be hard for Aunt March, but harder for us," Meg said with a laugh. "Jo is so terribly cross when she has to nurse her."

Just then they heard the front door slam. A moment later, Jo appeared in the doorway.

"Well, where have you been?" Meg asked, placing the poker back in the rack.

"Racketing about, as usual," Jo said. There was a queer look on her face. She glanced at Amy, then quickly took to dusting off her skirt.

"With Laurie, I suppose," Meg said with a sigh.

Laurie was their neighbor, Theodore Laurence, the grandson of the kind and courtly Mr. Laurence. He was a dear friend to each of the girls, but he and Jo were particularly close. Jo was the only one to call him "Teddy," and they were always tramping about the countryside, cooking up schemes and jokes.

"No, Teddy is 'grinding away,' as he says, with his books just now. I was on my own," Jo replied.

"What is it, Jo?" Beth asked. "You look as though you have something to tell us."

"Yes, your mouth is puckered up in that odd way, as though it were full of words you were holding back," Meg said with a smile.

"It's nothing much, just a story I've been working on," Jo said. "I've got my chores to take care of now, but once they're done you are all invited to the attic.

I do believe it's time for a special meeting of the March sisters."

"That would be capital," Meg said. "We always love to hear your stories."

"Yes, Jo," Amy piped up. "A dramatic tale is just what we need." Jo's stories were so good that one forgot everything else while one listened. And Amy would dearly love to forget her thoughts for a bit.

She had never kept a secret from her sisters before. But somehow she knew that, though her decision made perfect sense in her head, her sisters might see it differently. She'd rather avoid hearing their opinions. They were usually so *right*. It was awfully provoking.

"All right then, a special meeting it is," Jo said.

"With tea!" Beth proposed. "We'll carry up the tea tray and some buttered toast."

"An excellent notion," Jo said approvingly. "I'll see you there at half past."

Everyone flew through the rest of the housework, anxious to settle into the old, comfortable three-legged sofa in the garret to hear Jo's story. Meg and Beth made up the tea tray and carried the teapot, china, and toast up three flights of stairs. Amy plumped the pillows and unfolded the old quilts, for the attic was cold in November.

Soon they heard Jo's quick step on the stairs. She hurried in, the same peculiar expression on her face.

"Now, I haven't written this down as of yet, so you must bear with me if I stumble," Jo said, drawing the worn armchair closer to the sofa.

"We'll be patient," Meg said, setting a cup of hot tea by Jo's elbow.

With a slice of buttered toast in one hand and her teacup in the other, Amy settled back against the pillows.

"Well, now. Once upon a time," Jo began, "years and years ago, before the continents were settled and there was gaslight and grand cities, there lived a king who ruled a kingdom high on a mountaintop. This mountaintop was so near the moon and stars that it actually scraped the sky. And the stars provided enough illumination at night. They never needed candles or gaslight. In the kingdom there was a young storyteller, renowned for his tales, who was invited to the king's court one day. . . ." Jo went on.

Amy nibbled at her toast and sipped at her tea. She knew, by the way Jo had begun, that a fairy would appear in the story, and she liked Jo's fairy tales best. She liked to hear about kings and princesses, and fairies wearing gossamer gowns who wove glittering robes out of spiderwebs and drank sweet morning dew collected from bluebells.

"This story concerns a clever storyteller who held the royal court spellbound with one thrilling tale," began Jo. "All of the lords and ladies showered him with praise, and the king heaped gold and precious stones upon him for making the court such a gay place. Each night the storyteller would act out another chapter of his amazing story. Everyone hung on his words, gasping at the plot twists and laughing at the mad comic turns."

Amy hooked her pinky finger over her teacup, feeling very regal and courtly.

"But the man's days of glory were short-lived, for his troubles began when he arrived late at the castle one night with no story to tell! He recovered his wit the next day. But another night he was at a loss for a cliff-hanger. The poor chap had to race from the room!"

Beth, Amy, and Meg leaned closer to Jo, wondering what could be wrong.

Jo's voice deepened, as it usually did near a story's climax. In a dire tone, she revealed the truth. "In the darkness of the storyteller's chamber, we see a twinkling magic fairy who is furious! It turns out that the storyteller was a thief—a fraud who stole his enchanting story from the fairy. Each day, the fairy would tell him another chapter. That is, until the fairy discovered that the storyteller was using the tale to gain great wealth at the court."

Amy's toast felt scratchy and dry in her throat, and she hastily gulped her tea. She wasn't sure that she liked this story after all.

"What the fairy knew was that the storyteller did not trust his own talent," Jo said. "You see, even as a boy, he'd been praised for his skill at telling a good tale. But he did not feel he was quite good enough for the court. So he borrowed someone else's tale in order to have praise heaped upon his head. And he did get the praise, but . . ."

Jo's voice died away. Amy took another sip of tea. It was cold now.

"But what? What happened next, Jo?" Beth asked anxiously.

"Did the king throw him into the dungeon?" Meg asked.

Jo looked at Amy for the first time.

"I don't know what happens next," she said. "I was hoping that one of my sisters could help me with the ending."

Jo's eyes were so kind and honest that a lump rose in Amy's throat. She tried to swallow it, but the lump returned just as large as ever. She was afraid she would cry.

Jo knew!

She had seen Marmee's painting, and knew the mistake. Jo had made up the story just as a lesson for her!

"What do you think, Amy?" Jo prodded.

Meg and Beth looked at her with curious, innocent eyes. Shame washed over Amy, and she burst into tears. Her teacup shook against her saucer as she sobbed.

"What is it, dear?" Meg took the teacup from her hand. "Oh, my. Is it your head again?"

Beth knelt in front of the sofa. "Amy, what is the matter? Can we help?" She slipped her hand into Amy's.

Amy reached for the handkerchief in the pocket of her apron. "Jo thinks I'm horrid," she cried.

Meg gave Jo a reproachful look. "Jo would never think such a thing, dear. Tell her, Jo."

But Jo said nothing. She just waited, looking at Amy with love and compassion.

"She knows what I did," Amy said, in between sobs. "Not that it was my fault, exactly. I didn't know about the painting until I saw it on the wall. I promise!"

"What painting?" Meg asked.

"At the fair?" Beth prompted.

Pressing her handkerchief to her mouth, Amy sobbed out the story.

"I was so confused," she finished at last, wiping at the last tear. "I didn't know what to do at first. And Jenny Snow and May Chester were being so mean. They're saying that I'll lose to Adelaide Montgomery, and that it will serve me right. But I don't deserve to lose because of a mistake!"

"Of course you don't," Meg said sympathetically, patting her hand.

"It was all my fault! I was in such a hurry, and that confounded brown paper was so slippery," Jo said, full of remorse. "I should have checked the paintings again."

"It would have been hard at the fair to admit the mistake, with so many people around," Beth said.

Amy peeped at her sisters over her handkerchief. They were all staring at her expectantly.

"But what are you going to do now, dear?" Meg asked in her sweet way.

"Do?" Amy asked. "Why, nothing. I'm just going to have to bear this torture and this horrible guilt!" she cried dramatically, ending on a shuddering sob.

"But why, Amy?" Jo asked. "It's not too late. You

can withdraw the painting from the competition. Why don't you?"

Amy wiped at her fresh tears. "Because," she said, her chin wobbling. She forced her voice not to quaver. She was determined not to cry again.

She took a deep breath and faced her sisters. "I want to win the prize!"

CHAPTER SEVEN

A Meeting by the River

*M*eg, Jo, and Beth stared at her, shocked.
"You mean you would let everyone think that you'd painted Marmee's painting?" Jo asked, her face quite red.

Meg raised her eyebrows at Jo. Amy knew that Meg was warning Jo not to explode. She drew closer to Meg. Her oldest sister always protected her and took her part.

"Now, Amy," Meg said, patting her hand. "We know it wouldn't be easy to admit the mistake to Mrs. Lillipenny—"

"It would be dreadfully hard," Amy agreed, glad of Meg's support. "She'd think I'd done it on purpose. She'd think I'd crumbled from guilt! For why else would I withdraw the painting? And then everyone would think that I was dishonest. I'd be positively disgraced!"

"They wouldn't think such a thing!" Beth exclaimed, shocked. "It was an honest mistake."

"It was *my* honest mistake, and perhaps I should be the one to correct it," Jo said.

"No, Jo," Meg said, shaking her head. "This is Amy's decision. And she must make it," she added. "Marmee would say the same."

"I suppose you're right," Jo agreed.

Amy set her jaw stubbornly. "Well, then, it's settled. Because I've made it."

Meg and Jo exchanged a worried glance.

"I'm going to keep the painting in the competition," Amy said.

Both Jo and Meg frowned. Meg cleared her throat.

"Well, then," she said. "That's that, I suppose. We're not going to order you to withdraw the painting."

"Good," Amy said.

"But," Meg continued sternly, "we do want you to

think very carefully about this course. What would Marmee think?"

At that thought of Marmee, Amy wavered. But she pushed the thought of her mother's disappointment out of her head. She concentrated on how she'd feel when she stepped up to receive the blue ribbon while May and Jenny burned, and the rest of Concord applauded. She couldn't give that up!

"Marmee believes that it's best for everyone to make their own decisions and suffer the consequences," Meg said. "Even when the decision is wrong, or selfish."

"Which this decision is, young lady," Jo said. Her eyebrows bristled at Amy in that older-sister way that Amy detested.

Even Beth was looking at her sorrowfully. Amy shifted impatiently. It was bad enough that she knew her sisters disapproved. Did they have to show their disapproval so conspicuously?

They just didn't know what it was like to always be the poor girl at school. Amy had won friends, but it had been a hard battle. By winning the contest, she would show girls like Jenny and May that even poor Amy March was worthy of praise.

Wanting to avoid their troubled eyes, Amy glanced out the window. There was still some day-

light left, and the setting sun would cast interesting
shadows on the riverbank. How she longed to sit
quietly and sketch . . . and escape this tedious lectur-
ing from her sisters!

She stood. "Well, I'm going out for a walk," she
announced, trying to adopt a casual tone.

"Good. I hope you are going to think seriously
about your actions," Meg said severely.

"No," Amy said, lifting her chin in a way she
hoped conveyed a regal air. "I'm not going to think
at all. I'm going to sketch."

Tucking her sketch pad under her arm, Amy
headed for the riverbank. The rising wind made her
shiver. The slanting sun might have cast interesting
shadows, but the rays gave little warmth.

"I don't care," Amy said aloud. "I'm not going
back. Meg and Jo will just be bossy and disagreeable."

She tramped through the meadow, swinging her
sketch pad and telling herself that she was right, and
her sisters were wrong. A little solitude would do her
more good than heaps of lectures. But as she reached
the river, she discovered that someone was sitting in
her favorite sketching spot on the bank. With a start,
she realized it was Adelaide Montgomery.

Amy stopped in her tracks just as the girl turned around. Amy waited for Adelaide to lift her chin, or nod coolly, or turn away.

But instead, Adelaide gave a shy smile. "Hello," she called. "You don't have to go. I'm just sketching that old tree over there. I see you have your pad, too. Do sit down."

Amy sank down next to Adelaide. She felt odd, but she couldn't refuse Adelaide's request without seeming rude. She tried to see the girl's sketch pad, but it was angled away from her.

"You're Amy March," Adelaide said. "I've seen you at the Hall. But it's so crowded and everyone seems to know each other, and I never got up the nerve to say hello."

Why, Adelaide was shy! That was why she lifted her chin and avoided Amy's eyes that way!

Amy waggled into a more comfortable seat on the bank. "I suppose it's hard to move to a new place," she said.

"It's not so very hard," Adelaide said quickly, as though she didn't want to seem to complain. "My aunt tells me that everyone says that you're the best artist in your school."

"Everyone says that you're the best in Concord," Amy returned politely. "Though I'm sorry that I

haven't seen your work yet. There was such a crush
of people last evening, I had to go home or I would
have fainted dead away."

"I know what you mean," Adelaide said. "It was
frightfully hot. But I did see your paintings. You are
very talented."

Amy opened her sketchbook. It was nice of Adelaide to compliment her. But it almost felt to Amy
as though the girl was complimenting her as a
teacher might, instead of a girl her own age.

Adelaide drew a few lines on her pad. "I'm having
a beastly time of it with that old tree," she said.
"The branches seem so sad and yearning somehow,
as though they want to join the river's flow."

Amy looked over at the tree. She had sketched it
many times, but she'd never realized why she'd
found it so romantic. Adelaide had summed up her
own feelings.

"Why, that's just the way it looks!" she exclaimed.
"As though the tree wanted to be swept away toward
the sea." She took out her pencils. She'd dearly love
to capture such a mood.

Amy drew a few quick lines to capture the leaning
trunk and graceful branches. For a few minutes, both
girls were silent, and the only sound was the scratch
of pencil against paper.

Amy shaded in a drooping branch. "May Chester says that your father is a famous artist in New York," she said.

Adelaide nodded. "He paints portraits. He does all the society ladies. That's why he has to live in New York. All his commissions are there. He would dearly love to live in Boston, so I could be with him."

"But couldn't you live with him in New York?" Amy asked. She regretted the question immediately when a flush rose on Adelaide's pale cheek.

"He only has a studio, you see, and it wouldn't be a proper place for me to grow up," Adelaide said. "He hopes to make a home and send for me soon. Until then, I have to live with my Aunt Anna Manderly. She begged to take me in after my mother died. My father only agreed because Aunt Manderly is so good, and intelligent, and loves art as much as we do. She plans to take me on a grand tour of Europe one day."

"Is your aunt the lady you were with when you dropped off your painting?" Amy asked. She felt slightly puzzled. The lady had been dressed so shabbily. How could she afford such a trip?

Adelaide trained her eyes on the tree across the river. "Yes," she said quickly, "Aunt Manderly is of an artistic temperament. She lives simply and doesn't believe in fuss and finery. She devotes herself to higher things, to art and culture. That's why I am to study at home. She knows more than many art teachers. My father has complete confidence in her. Papa is very particular about my education. He thinks I have a genius for art. Papa says we'll both live in Paris, when I am old enough."

A pang of jealousy shot through Amy. "What a thrilling, romantic family!" she exclaimed. "I long to go to Paris and Rome. You are so lucky!"

"Yes, I know," Adelaide said.

Amy had supposed that getting to know Adelaide would cause her to feel more guilty about her deception. But to her surprise, it had the opposite effect. After all, Adelaide had so many advantages. She had a thrillingly romantic family, a famous artist for a father, and an aunt who was determined to teach her about art. And her family thought she was a genius.

In short, Adelaide didn't *need* the prize the way Amy did!

Amy bent over her sketch pad again. *Adelaide gets to live in Paris when she's older,* she thought enviously. *Why should she care about a pokey old contest?*

Amy added to her sketch, but the sun was lower now, and it was difficult to see. She should go back home for the early dinner. Besides, she wouldn't want to antagonize Jo and Meg any more than she had already.

She closed her sketchbook. "I'll be late if I don't hurry," she said. "Will you be at the fair tonight?"

"No, I'm afraid not," Adelaide said. "I'm needed at home. But I'll be there tomorrow." She jumped up. "It *is* late," she said in a worried tone. "Aunt Manderly will scold me."

She hurriedly bent to pick up her sketchbook. But it slipped through her fingers and landed by Amy's hand. Amy picked it up and flipped through a few pages.

In an abrupt gesture, Adelaide reached out and snatched it back. "My best sketches are at home. And I really must be going," she said pointedly.

"I'm sorry," Amy murmured. "Goodbye, Adelaide."

The girl thrust the sketchbook under her arm. "Goodbye," she said, and hurried away.

Thoughtfully, Amy tucked her own sketchbook under her arm. Adelaide had snatched back the pad, but not before Amy had stolen a quick look at the page.

The sketch was so badly done!

And the one on the previous page had been worse.

Puzzled, Amy started across the meadow toward home. Perhaps Adelaide's painting was much better than her drawing. Or perhaps Jenny and May were stirring up trouble, and Adelaide wasn't very good at all.

It all added to the girl's mystery. But Amy decided one thing. That evening, when she went to the fair, the first thing she would do would be to find Adelaide's painting.

CHAPTER EIGHT

Rivals

*L*ater that evening Amy stared at her reflection in Marmee's mirror. It was too awful that she had to wear her pink and white school dress again tonight, but she was saving her best gown for Saturday night. It was the most splendid color, a rose so deep it was almost purple, and Laurie had promised her a small bouquet of pink rosebuds to pin on her sash.

Unless Jo told Laurie what had happened with Marmee's painting. Amy frowned. She would hate it if Laurie became as cross and gloomy as her sisters. He would most likely forget her rosebuds, but even worse, he wouldn't congratulate her or make a fuss over her. And Laurie was so delightful when making fusses over people! Amy had been looking forward to it, and it would be very bad of Jo to spoil her pleasure.

Amy smoothed the skirt of her dress. Jo, Meg, and Beth were waiting for her in the parlor. All afternoon they'd had the most serious faces on, as though they were heading for a hanging instead of a gay winter fair.

Well, she wouldn't let them spoil her pleasure. Amy gave a final smooth to the lace on her cuffs, then headed downstairs to her sisters.

"Amy, you've dawdled so long you missed most of Marmee's letter," Meg told her. "It came with the evening post. Jo was just reading it aloud."

Amy took her place on the sofa. "I'll read the earlier parts afterward," she said. "Go on, Jo."

Jo returned to the letter. " 'Ella is growing stronger by the day, so I have no more worries and can enjoy my time pleasantly enough,' " she read. " 'But I miss my little women. I'm afraid that I talk of you all far too much for Ella's sweet patience! Thank you for your letters, and I send all my love back to you. I trust that each of you will continue to be the good, loving girls I am so very proud of."

Jo's eyes rose above the letter and met Amy's. Meg shook her head in a sad fashion.

Oh, bother! Amy thought. *I don't know how I shall be able to bear these looks!*

She stood. "We'd better be going. I'll get my bonnet."

Amy stood in front of the mirror and tied her bonnet strings with a jerk. She tried to feel pleasure in her pretty dress and the evening to come. But the thought of her sisters kept interfering.

She stamped her foot. "I won't *let* myself be unhappy!" she told her reflection. "I won't!"

As soon as they stepped into the Exhibition Hall, the March girls were caught up in the throng. All of Concord seemed to have turned out that evening. Meg, Jo, Beth, and Amy moved slowly through the crowd, gazing in admiration at the evergreen boughs hung down the hall in garlands, the glittering sconces, and the array of goods displayed on white tablecloths. Slowly their faces brightened.

"Will you look at all this richness, girls!" Jo exclaimed. "I declare, it's enough to tempt a monk."

Amy felt her spirits rise. At last her sisters were

jolly again! Beth's soft eyes sparkled, Meg's head was held high with her usual sweet grace, and Jo walked with a quick, excited step.

But as they strolled through the exhibits, friends and neighbors approached to greet them, and they all had a word or two of praise for Amy's entries in the exhibition.

"Those hollyhocks!" Mrs. Arden exclaimed. "To the life, they were!"

"Did you realize that you girls had a genius in your midst?" Mr. Lamb teased, his blue eyes twinkling.

"My, oh, my. Little Amy is quite a treasure!" Mrs. Wilmott cried, wringing her plump hands. "I thought I could positively smell those hollyhocks!"

Each time someone praised her, her sisters reacted so oddly! Meg pursed her lips in a strained smile. Beth shrank back and looked at the tips of her boots. Jo's eyebrows bristled, and her answer was always a sharp, "Yes, we never know what our Amy will do!"

Amy wanted to enjoy the praise. But a weight on her heart was growing. The gaslights seemed dimmer, and the bright colors of dresses and flowers did not look as gay as they had the evening before.

I will not let myself be unhappy! Amy told herself

again. *What I'm doing isn't so very wrong, and they are mean to make me feel so badly about it.*

Amy determined to act the part of a happy, contented girl. So the more troubled her heart grew, the wider her smiles became, and the more lively her behavior. She would not allow her sisters to have the satisfaction of dimming her spirits.

But she was almost unmasked from her bright pose when Mr. Laurence and Laurie approached. Laurie made a grand bow in front of her.

"Two masterpieces! My humble admiration is yours, Miss March. You have brought spring in November, and hollyhocks are now my favorite flower."

Jo frowned. "Oh, why must you bow in that ridiculous fashion, Teddy?" she said. "Amy has had quite enough praise, I assure you."

The merriment faded in Laurie's black eyes, and he looked at Jo, puzzled. It wasn't like Jo not to join in praise of her sisters. But Mr. Laurence, who hadn't heard the exchange, moved forward and took Amy's hand.

"I am charmed, Miss Amy," he told her in his courtly fashion. "You have a great talent for one so young."

"Thank you, Mr. Laurence," Amy murmured.

Somehow, her neighbor's grave admiration had made her feel worse than Laurie's extravagance.

"I—I promised Kitty I would meet her," Amy said, stumbling over the words. "I'll find you all later."

She hurried away through the crowd. If she could only get away from her family, Amy decided, she could finally enjoy herself!

She saw Kitty making her way past pots of bright yellow roses. Kitty reached out to steady a pot as she almost knocked one over. She caught Amy looking at her, and she made a comical grimace and waved Amy over.

Kitty's face lit up as Amy joined her. "You should hear what Jenny and May have begun," she said, squeezing her arm. "They are telling all the girls that you are crushed and in despair that Adelaide is a better artist! They've told everyone that you and Adelaide are rivals. Oh, I can't wait until you win! You'll show them."

"How can I be in despair, when I haven't even seen Adelaide's painting?" Amy said scornfully.

"It's over there, next to that pillar," Kitty said, pointing. "Now I must go meet my mother. Come and tell me what you think after you see it. We'll be at the booth with the painted vases. Oh, dear, I hope I won't knock one over!"

Kitty hurried away, and Amy went off in the direction she had indicated. She slipped next to the pillar, searching for Adelaide's name by the different works. There it was, next to a painting in a thin gold frame.

Amy turned to stone as she gazed at the painting. It was a lovely picture of the Concord town square in late summer. The shimmering greens of the trees and the blue of the sky made the painting seem to float against the white wall.

But it wasn't the excellence of the work that took her breath away.

The painting was a fraud!

Amy clearly remembered the day in September when she'd walked through the square with Meg. They had seen an artist at work, and had stopped to admire his canvas.

She would never forget the painting she had seen that day, for she had greatly admired it. The artist had captured the hazy summer light and the dappled shadows from the flickering green leaves. On a stone bench sat a small, black Scottie, a red ribbon round its neck. The dog had a dignified posture, as if he felt he had a perfect right to be there.

She had laughed aloud at the dog, and the painter

had smiled. She would never forget it. And now here was the same painting, right in front of her!

Adelaide had lied!

Turning, Amy rushed through the crowd to find her sisters. She came upon them at the flower booth, where Beth was admiring the roses.

"You won't believe what I've discovered," Amy whispered to them. "I saw Adelaide Montgomery's painting, and it is a fraud! It's the work of a professional painter. Do you remember that day in September, Meg, when we saw the artist painting the town square? It's the very same painting! Adelaide never painted it at all!"

"Are you certain, Amy?" Jo looked doubtful. "Adelaide could have painted the same scene. You've sketched the town square yourself. Or perhaps she copied the painting."

"No, it's the same painting," Amy declared. "That black Scottie dog is sitting on the bench, still looking so comical. He has exactly the same expression in his eyes."

"I remember the painting well," Meg said. "Do you think Adelaide submitted as her own?"

"Of course she did!" Amy said scornfully. "It's a dreadful, dreadful lie. I know that Adelaide didn't paint that painting! I saw her sketches, and they're terrible. She doesn't have any talent—except the skills of a thief!"

Jo, Meg, and Beth exchanged a glance. Amy's own words echoed in her head, and she knew what her sisters were thinking but would not say. They looked at her, and on each of their faces was a question that she did not want to answer.

They thought she was just as dreadful as Adelaide!

CHAPTER NINE

Good Works

"*O*h, dear," Meg fretted the next morning. She sat at Marmee's desk, leafing through the various papers and books there. "I'm afraid I've misplaced the note that Marmee left. It lists all the families to whom I'm to bring the food baskets."

"I'll help you look," Amy suggested, putting down her sewing. Today, she would be as helpful as she could, so that she wouldn't receive more head shaking and sad looks.

"Oh, better not, we'll just confuse things more," Meg said with a sigh.

"Beth and I are almost finished making up the baskets," Jo announced, popping her head into the parlor.

"They won't do a bit of good if I can't find the names of the families," Meg said, searching the cubbyholes of the desk.

"Try checking Marmee's ledger," Jo suggested. "Perhaps you tucked the note in there."

Meg opened the leather-bound book. "Oh, glory! Here it is. Good work, Jo."

"Beth and I will finish up, then. Do you want me to come with you?" Jo asked.

"Amy will come," Meg decided. She looked toward the corner where Amy was hemming napkins.

Amy kept her eyes on her work. "Yes, Meg," she said obediently.

"The fresh air will do you good, Amy," Jo said. "Beth is planning to help Hannah with the bread baking, and I'm off to dust the upstairs after I load the baskets. Is Mr. Laurence sending the carriage for you?"

Mr. Laurence made the generous loan of his carriage whenever he could, especially when Marmee distributed food baskets on Saturdays.

"Yes, bless him," Meg said. "Oh, I hear it now.

Amy, perhaps you could help Jo carry the baskets to the carriage."

It took only a few minutes to load the carriage with the wicker hampers. Dressed in their warmest cloaks and bonnets, Meg and Amy climbed into the carriage, which took off with a lurch.

As they jounced along the rutted road, Amy decided that she was grateful that Meg had pressed her into service. At least if she lost herself in good works, she didn't have to think about what to do about Adelaide Montgomery. Should she tattle, and expose Adelaide's lie? She'd have to expose herself, too.

Amy had puzzled over the right thing to do all night long, and all morning, too. And still she couldn't figure out what was right!

"There," Meg said as she swung the carriage door closed. "Only one more home to go to. Oh, Amy, doesn't it break your heart to see such poverty? It makes me grateful for my blessings."

"It seems so little to bring, when there is so much want," Amy said, glancing at the baskets with a sigh.

"That is why we must do all we can, and be grateful for what we have ourselves," Meg said, patting her hand. She peered at the last name on the list.

"This family is new to our list," she said. "Would you mind taking this last basket in, dear? I confess I'm done in."

"I don't mind," Amy said, as Meg leaned her head against the upholstered seat with a sigh. "What did you say their name was?"

"It's a Mrs. Manderly—an elderly woman who recently took in a ward," Meg answered.

Manderly! Amy started at the name. But it couldn't be Adelaide's aunt. Adelaide had implied that her aunt was well off.

The carriage drew up in front of a small home with a sagging front porch. Paint was peeling off the shutters.

This can't be Adelaide's house, Amy thought. *It certainly doesn't look as if the daughter of a famous artist lives here.*

She picked up the basket and walked down the path. When she knocked on the door, the same tall, stern woman she had seen at the Hall opened the door.

"Good morning," Amy said. She held up the food basket. "I've brought—"

"Shhh," Mrs. Manderly warned. She closed the door halfway and whispered to Amy, "I've a guest inside. Can you bring the basket around to the kitchen? I left the door off the latch."

"I'd be glad to," Amy said politely. The door was shut abruptly.

She crossed the yard to the side of the house and pushed open the door. She found herself in a small, tidy kitchen.

Taking a quick look around, Amy noted that the larder looked empty. And there wasn't much coal in the scuttle. The air felt almost as chilly as outside.

Amy placed the basket on the scrubbed wooden table. The sound of voices penetrated through the door, and she heard the name "Adelaide."

She knew it was wrong to eavesdrop. But Amy couldn't resist drifting toward the door to listen, just for a moment. The mystery of why Adelaide seemed to live so poorly when her picture of her life was so different was just too tempting to ignore.

"I'm so glad you were able to stop in on your way to Boston, Harriet," she heard Mrs. Manderly say.

"You seem to have been busy since last you wrote," her guest replied. "You've taken in an orphan?"

"Yes, my ward, Adelaide Montgomery," Mrs. Manderly replied. "Oh, do have another cup of tea. Adelaide calls me 'aunt,' though I am only a second cousin once removed, on her mother's side. Her mother died quite suddenly this past summer, and

someone needed to take the poor girl in. She was destitute."

"And the father?" the visitor asked. "Can't he care for the child?"

"He can barely care for himself," Mrs. Manderly replied. "Orson Montgomery is his name. Perhaps you have heard the name, for he is a painter of some note, though little income. He abandoned the family when Adelaide was barely two. He could not support a family, and could not give up being a painter. So he chose to run away, though I do think he loved his wife. Now he barely makes enough to keep a roof over his head. But when Adelaide's mother died, he was forced to provide for his daughter at last."

"He wouldn't take her in?"

"No, he decided she was better off here, and I'm sure that he was right," Mrs. Manderly said. "I have my odd ways, but I do care for the girl, poor thing. Orson Montgomery came here in September to beg for my help, and of course I could not refuse. She came to me a few weeks later, but her father has not returned to visit her, not even once! He has put off the visit time and again. I think his intentions are good, but good intentions don't make a good parent. I thought the poor girl's heart would break when he failed to show up a fortnight ago."

"So he does not contribute to the household? That must be hard on you, to have another mouth to feed." Amy heard the note of disapproval in the visitor's voice.

"It has not been easy, I must confide," Mrs. Manderly said. "I have a small income, and it only stretches so far. Orson had promised to send money every month, and does so on an irregular schedule. He pens a few lines to Adelaide and sends his love, but I fear the child feels the lack of his presence keenly. He's never had to act as a father before, you see, so he doesn't know how to go about it."

"How sad it all is. What will happen to the girl? Can you get her any schooling, or have her learn a trade?"

"Schooling is expensive, and we shall have to see about a trade," Mrs. Manderly said. "She's just turned twelve. It would help if she had a talent or skill, but I'm afraid her mother did not teach her one. Her sewing is atrocious, and she can't do needlework. I had some hopes that she had inherited her father's talent, but it was a vain one. No, Adelaide has no talents and little beauty. Worst of all, the girl is exceptionally bright. You know that often scares a suitor off rather than attracts him."

The other voice was as dry as old parchment. "I am afraid I am well acquainted with the contradiction, Anna."

Mrs. Manderly sighed. "I fear she shall have a hard path to walk in the world. I will do what I can, but my resources are small. She's had an unlucky past, and her future looks bleak."

Amy pressed her hand to her mouth. She couldn't bear to hear another word. Shocked and dismayed, she rushed out of the house.

CHAPTER TEN

The Best Thing to Do

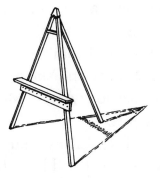

*A*delaide Montgomery was a liar, Amy thought on the way home. She had lied about her home, and her father's love, and she had submitted a painting that wasn't hers.

But in the bare kitchen of the Manderly house, Amy had gained a glimpse of the lonely desperation that must have prompted those lies. Adelaide's plight had touched her heart. What must it be like to have a father who claimed to care, yet couldn't quite manage to visit you? Amy's own father was far away in

Washington, but he wrote once a week to the family. In addition, he sent individual letters to each of his girls, filled with information and jokes that were especially meant for them.

Outside, the horse's hooves clicked in a steady rhythm. Amy pulled her cape closer, wondering what Father was doing at that moment. But she was certain that he was thinking of his family as often as they were thinking of him.

"Now that we're quiet and snug, would you mind if I asked you a question, Amy?" Meg asked, breaking into her thoughts.

"Of course not, Meg," Amy said, for Meg's tone was warm and sweet, as it had been before this terrible trial. And after hearing about Adelaide's sad history, she was more inclined to treasure her sisters, no matter that they plagued her occasionally.

"How will you feel if Marmee's hollyhock drawing does take first prize?" Meg asked gently. She slipped her gloved hand into Amy's and squeezed it. "You take such pride in your work, dear, as well you should. You are a fine artist. But perhaps pride is misplaced when desperation is a part of it."

"Desperation?" Amy asked.

"Perhaps I spoke too strongly," Meg said slowly. "But it does seem as though you're pinning your hopes on a grand prize in order to prove something to others. Jo tried to tell you that with her fairy story. You don't trust your own gift to bring you the rewards you yearn for. And I don't mean garnet rings or pearl necklaces or blue ribbons," Meg added.

"What *do* you mean?" Amy asked.

"What you really yearn for is acceptance and praise and love," Meg said. "Just as all of us do, I suppose. But that makes me sad, for it means you don't realize that you have all of those things already. You don't know how very much you're treasured by those who love you. I see a fall ahead for you, dearest, because I don't think that the grand prize will make you happy. Rewards lose their sweetness when they are undeserved."

Amy stared at her sister. How strange that Meg should read her thoughts! And how strange that both she and Adelaide should share so much. She hadn't thought she was like the girl at all. But if Adelaide's deception was born of desperation, Amy's own need was a shadow of the same emotion. She had felt desperate to prove her value.

And here Meg was pointing out how loved and cherished she already was!

Amy returned Meg's squeeze. "You're the best sister in the world, Meg," she told her. "I haven't decided what I shall do yet. Can you wait, and trust that I'll choose for the best?"

"Of course I can, dear," Meg answered.

I want to help Adelaide somehow, Amy wrote in her journal. *I miss Father dreadfully, and yet I know he is thinking of me and wants to be home as much as we want him to be here. And he writes so often, I have no fear that he would ever forget me. I feel his love from far away.*

But what must Adelaide feel? No wonder she makes up stories! She wants what she cannot have—a father who shows his love in as many ways as he can.

Perhaps that is the reason she wants so badly to win the contest! She wants to tell him that she got the grand prize. She wants him to be proud of her. And maybe she thinks he will love her more.

Amy sketched an easel in her book. What had Meg said? *"Rewards lose their sweetness if they are undeserved."*

Wouldn't Adelaide feel that way, too?

So what was the best thing to do?

1. *Call on Adelaide, and confess my mistake about Marmee's painting.*
2.

Amy hesitated, thinking of her options. But there was no number two. The right thing to do was to talk to Adelaide.

Once I confess, Adelaide will do the same. She'll tell me of her own deception. We shall both withdraw our works—and we shall become good friends.

Amy closed her journal, satisfied. There would be a happy ending, after all.

Glancing at the clock, Amy sprang to her feet. The prizes were to be awarded that evening.

She didn't have much time.

Her walk to the Manderly home was long and muddy, but soon she was knocking on the door once again.

This time, Mrs. Manderly opened the door wider. She nodded at Amy, surprised.

"Good afternoon, Mrs. Manderly," Amy said. "May I speak to Adelaide? My name is Amy March."

"Of course, Miss March," Mrs. Manderly said. "I'll fetch her for you."

The parlor held a worn sofa, an armchair, and a desk. But the sofa was no more shabby than the Marches', and the room was clean and bright. The wood gleamed from good care, and there was a small but cheerful fire in the grate.

Amy perched on a chair. In only a moment Adelaide entered the room. Amy jumped up again.

"Adelaide, I've come to see you to make a confession," Amy blurted. "There's been a dreadful mistake."

Adelaide looked surprised. "Mistake?"

"My sister Jo helped me pack my paintings for the fair," Amy explained. "But things were confused, and one of my mother's paintings was slipped in the folder. It's the painting of the hollyhocks. Mrs. Lillipenny thought it was mine and put it in the show. But it isn't."

Adelaide frowned. "And why are you telling me?"

"Because I'm not sure what to do," Amy said. "I thought perhaps you could help me. It's not fair to submit someone else's painting and call it your own. Don't you agree?"

"No, it isn't fair," Adelaide said coolly. "But I think

Mrs. Lillipenny is the one to talk to about it, don't you?"

Frustrated, Amy squeezed her hands together. She was sure that once she'd confessed, Adelaide would do the same!

"But I didn't mean to do wrong, you see," Amy continued. "I think everyone will understand, and be kind."

Adelaide lifted one shoulder in a shrug. "I suppose."

This isn't working at all! Amy thought frantically. She would have to force a confession, after all.

"Adelaide, I know that you didn't do that painting," she burst out. "I came to help you make things right."

Amy waited, her eyes trained on Adelaide. There was a flush on the girl's pale cheeks, but Adelaide sat as still as ever, frozen in the same polite position.

"I'm sure I don't know what you mean, Amy," Adelaide said.

Amy's mouth dropped open in surprise. She'd been sure that Adelaide would burst into a storm of remorse. But the girl just sat there, as cool as you please!

"Adelaide, it's no good to pretend," Amy said kindly. "You see, I saw the artist who painted it on the town square. It's the identical painting, with the black dog. I'm certain of it."

Adelaide's mouth tightened. For a moment, she sat without moving a muscle. Then her chin lifted, and her gray eyes flashed.

"All right, I didn't paint it," she said defiantly. "My father did. But why shouldn't I take credit for his work? I'm sure I shall be as good as he is one day, for he is always telling me so. Each week when he comes to see me, he looks at my sketches."

"He comes to see you every week," Amy repeated.

"That's right," Adelaide said proudly. "Papa and I are as close as father and daughter can be."

Amy didn't have the heart to tell Adelaide that she knew that was a lie, too. Adelaide couldn't admit the truth even to herself. She wanted to have a doting father, so she invented one.

How sad it all is, Mrs. Manderly's friend had said. Amy felt the same way.

Some of the pity must have shown in her eyes, for Adelaide suddenly shot to her feet. Her face was pale and set. Her gray eyes were now like chips of ice.

"Do what you want, Miss March," Adelaide said in a remote tone. "Tell the world about my secret, for I will not. I will not withdraw my painting. And

I suggest that you do not, either. Why should we, at this late date? The best painting shall win the prize. Now, it is almost teatime, and I have chores to do. Good day."

What could Amy do but leave? Murmuring a goodbye, she slipped out of the house.

Amy walked home slowly, more confused and upset than when she had left. She was no closer to a decision than before, she realized. Adelaide had only made her dilemma more complicated!

Adelaide deserved a prize even less than Amy did. No matter how sad and lonely she was, she had no right to lie.

But was it the right thing to expose her? Especially if Amy would benefit. Even if she withdrew Marmee's painting, she would still have one in the fair. Without Adelaide as competition, she would most likely win. Justice would be served, in a fashion. Amy would get an easel, and enough money for the pretty garnet ring she wanted, as well as a replacement for Meg's cameo.

But would that be justice? Would it be right? Adelaide would be left with worse than nothing, for her reputation would be soiled. Who would want to be friends with her once they knew the truth?

Amy would get her garnet and her glory. That had been all she'd wanted a few weeks ago.

But something had changed. She had been trying to figure out a way to get what she wanted, and make it seem right in her own mind. That had involved quite a bit of twisting and turning, Amy had to admit. Now all she wanted was to do what was right for everybody.

"The right path can be the hardest one," Marmee told her once. "But it's usually the clearest."

"Not this time, Marmee," Amy whispered. "I wish you were here to help me find it!"

CHAPTER ELEVEN

Ribbons and Decisions

*I*n the Exhibition Hall that evening, Amy nervously smoothed the skirt of her best gown. She fingered the rosebuds on her sash, happy that Laurie had remembered to send them. She thought of his kindness and Meg's quiet words: *You don't realize how very much you're treasured by those who love you.* That gave her the courage to walk toward the Young Artists' Exhibition, her steps sure and purposeful.

Adelaide looked quietly elegant in a plain dress of dark blue with a simple black ribbon around her neck. Her head was held high as she stood in front of her father's painting. That told Amy without words that Adelaide had not changed her mind.

But it didn't matter, because Amy had made up her own mind. The judges were to begin their review of the art in a few minutes. There wasn't a moment to spare. Gathering her courage, she headed straight for Mrs. Lillipenny.

As she passed Adelaide, Amy saw the girl start. In Adelaide's gray eyes Amy saw fear and desperation. Perhaps she was afraid of what Amy might do, knowing the true artist behind Adelaide's work. A few words to Mrs. Lillipenny could cause a terrible scandal.

Then the girl lifted her head even higher, as if her pride wouldn't let her acknowledge the truth. Her lips curved in a cool smile, though Amy knew that Adelaide wasn't calm. She was just practiced at hiding a heart full of pain.

Amy marched up to Mrs. Lillipenny. "Excuse me, Mrs. Lillipenny," she said firmly. "I need to talk to you."

Later that evening when Amy saw her sisters threading through the crowd, she relaxed and smiled in relief. They were late, and she was beginning to wonder if they would come at all.

"We're so sorry, Amy," Meg said, hurrying over to her and kissing her cheek. "The kittens got out, and Beth couldn't leave until we found them because it's such a raw night. And then—"

"Jo misplaced her gloves—" Beth put in.

"—as I usually do, but Beth found them in my workbasket, which is odd, since they don't need mending," Jo said, with a comical air that made Amy laugh. "But by then we were late, so—"

"We decided to walk up to the Laurences and ride over with Laurie," Meg said breathlessly, "but they were dining at the Lambs, so we had to walk over, anyway."

"But we're here at last," Beth finished. "Did we miss anything?"

Amy stood aside. Hung on her painting of the weeping willow by the river was the second place pink ribbon.

"Second place!" Meg cried. "Well, I call that fine!"

"Good show, Amy," Jo declared. "But where is Marmee's painting?"

"I withdrew it from the competition," Amy told them. "Mrs. Lillipenny was very kind about the mistake." She peered at her sisters. "Are you relieved?"

"Not at all, for we knew you'd do what was right in the end," Jo said, beaming at her.

"Of course you would," Beth said, squeezing Amy's hand. "Who got first, Amy?"

"Adelaide Montgomery," Amy answered.

Her three sisters stared at her, surprised.

"You mean you didn't say anything?" Meg asked in a low voice. "But she didn't paint it!"

"I'll set things right, if you're afraid to make a fuss," Jo offered.

"No, Jo," Amy said. "I'm not afraid to do it. I just think it would be wrong. You see, I've thought and I've thought about this, and I think—I hope—that I did right. Coming face to face with Adelaide's lie made me see mine more clearly. I couldn't go through with it. But she could."

"But why don't you tell Mrs. Lillipenny that Adelaide lied?" Jo asked. "The girl doesn't deserve the prize."

"I suppose not," Amy said. "But that's her lesson to learn, isn't it? Didn't you and Meg leave me alone to learn my own lesson?"

Meg smiled at her. "That's quite true."

"But it's not very sporting of you to throw our lessons back in our faces," Jo said with a grin.

"Are you very disappointed, Amy?" Beth asked

sympathetically. "I know you wanted to take first place."

"I'm content with second, no matter how Jenny Snow jeers at me, for I know in my heart I did the right thing," Amy said solemnly. "I discovered that Adelaide has a very sad life. She is dreadfully poor, poorer than we are. And she loves her father, and he doesn't visit her or seem to care about her very much. I have so much more than she has! I'm happy I have talent, but I'm even happier that I have Father and Marmee and my sisters. So I decided that if Adelaide felt she needed to win, I couldn't be the one to stop her. Instead, I'm going to help her all I can."

"That's my girl," said Meg, who gave Amy a heartfelt hug.

Beth glanced at Adelaide. "I doubt she'll enjoy her prize," she remarked. "She doesn't look very happy."

Amy turned toward Adelaide, who stood alone in the middle of the laughing, chattering crowd. Beth was right. There was no mistaking the sad curve of her lips. Adelaide could not maintain that superior smile any longer.

For a moment, Amy thought that Adelaide looked over at her and her sisters with longing. But Adelaide quickly turned away again.

"Oh, dear, she looks lonely, doesn't she?" Jo said, always just as quick to soften as to fly into an irritable flurry. "I'm sorry to hear her life is hard. Let's invite her to take lemonade with us," Jo suggested. "I know she told a lie, and she has won the prize that our Amy should have received. But perhaps if we 'March her up' she'll learn that dishonesty never works in the end."

"It's a lesson I had to learn myself," Amy admitted. She grinned mischievously at Jo. "And you know how bad I am at lessons."

Laughing, Jo reached out to hug her. "I'm proud of you, my girl. I think you learned this one splendidly."

"Yes," Amy said with a sigh. "Tonight I learned to climb the *integra-tree*."

Meg looped her arm through Amy's. "That's *integrity*," she corrected gently. "And yes, dear, sometimes it can be a very steep climb."

Amy glanced over at Adelaide's painting and then examined her own. "I think it all worked out for the best, and I'm quite content," she told her sisters. "The best painting did win, after all."

"And if you ask me, you got the grand prize," Meg told her.

"Now let's go sweep the girl up," Jo said cheerfully. "All this wise talk has given me a thirst.

Jo started off, but Amy put a hand on her arm. "Wait, Jo," she said quietly. "Let me go."

Amy held out her new box of paints to Adelaide. The girl stared at her, startled.

"What's this?"

"I thought you might want to see them," Amy said. "They're quite wonderful. So many lovely colors . . . look," Amy said, opening the box.

Adelaide turned her head. "I suppose you think you deserve the easel."

"No," Amy said. "But I was hoping that you'd want to share the paints with me. We can go back to the riverbank and try to paint that old tree again. I never did get it right."

Slowly Adelaide turned her head. "You're inviting me to go sketching with you?" she asked. Disbelief and caution were mingled in her voice. And maybe . . . yearning?

Amy nodded. "I don't often meet other girls who love to draw as much as I do."

"But I cheated you!" Adelaide burst out.

"I don't see it that way," Amy said. She closed the paintbox firmly. "I think you cheated yourself. But I can't know all of your reasons, so I suppose it's not my concern. Unless you make it so," Amy added softly. "Because I'd be glad to listen. And . . . be your friend."

Suddenly a sheen of tears appeared in Adelaide's extraordinary gray eyes. "I think I would like to be your friend, Amy March," she said softly. "I don't think I've ever really had one. I'm not sure how to begin."

"Oh, that's the easy part," Amy said, her blue eyes twinkling. "We'll begin with lemonade!"

CHAPTER TWELVE

Sweet Home

*O*ne week later, Jo hurried into the parlor. "Steady, girls," she whispered. "The carriage just pulled up. Marmee's home!"

The four of them lined up in the parlor, their arms filled with the flowers Laurie had snatched from his uncle's glassed-in hothouse. Suppressed giggles were hushed, and four faces turned toward the parlor door.

They heard the carriage stop, and then the sound of Marmee's footsteps on the porch. Marmee knocked her boots against the stonework so that she wouldn't track in snow. The door opened.

"Girls? I'm home!" she called.

Amy suppressed a giggle. Jo poked her with an elbow and made a fierce face that cried, *Be quiet!*

"Girls?"

The wood floor creaked outside the parlor door. The knob turned, the door swung open, and there was Marmee, still in her cloak and bonnet.

"Welcome home, Marmee!" they cried in unison.

Marmee's hand flew to her mouth in surprise as she beheld four rosy faces over the fragrant blooms.

"Bless me, what a homecoming!" she said, laughing. She hurried toward them and tried to hug them all at the same time. She may have crushed a few flowers in the process, but no one minded at all.

"How I have missed these faces," Marmee said, stepping back to gaze at each of them individually. Then she kissed them, one by one.

"Not near as much as we missed you, I'd warrant," Jo told her.

They piled the flowers in her arms. Jo took Marmee's bonnet and cloak, and Meg led her to her favorite seat in the corner. Beth helped her off with her wet boots. Her slippers had been warmed by the fire, and Marmee slipped her stockinged feet into them with a sigh of contentment.

"Everything looks so shiny and clean," she said approvingly as she gazed around the room, pleasure in her eyes. "And the flowers are so lovely!" She bent down to smell them in her lap. "I suppose I should put them in a vase, but I can't bear to part with them yet."

"They are from Mr. Laurence and Laurie, of course," Meg told her.

"That boy!" Marmee said fondly. "The Laurences are far too generous. How happy I am to be home!"

"We made gingersnaps for tea," Amy told her. "And there's the loveliest chicken roasting in the oven for supper. And biscuits, and potatoes, and a whole crock of sweet butter. A treat for your first night home, Marmee. Hannah has been in the kitchen all morning."

"And the miracle is, she's not a bit cross," Jo said with a laugh.

"I declare, I've landed in paradise," Marmee said, smiling at her. "Cousin Ella's cook couldn't hold a candle to our Hannah."

"Tell us all the news," Meg said, sitting on the sofa. "How is Cousin Ella and the baby?"

"Both flourishing, thank heaven," Marmee told

them. "I left them in good hands. Oh, and your presents were so thoughtful, and brought such joy! I almost burst all my buttons with pride when I saw the care and thoughtfulness that went into that package."

"Did the baby like the doll?" Beth asked shyly.

"I think she did, though she couldn't say so," Marmee said thoughtfully. "It was so soft and dressed so prettily in that lovely linen smock. The baby snuggled up next to it in her cradle. And Ella put the slippers on as soon as she opened the package, and was so touched that she cried into Jo's handkerchiefs!"

The girls all laughed with delight at the picture.

"I'm glad we could be there in spirit," Meg said, satisfied.

Marmee smiled at them. "Now, what about my little women? You look well and happy, but I can't believe my chicks didn't get into a scrape or two while I was away."

Amy knew better than to glance at any of her sisters. Meg and Jo had told her that they would keep her story secret, if she wished it. Marmee need never know that her drawing had been entered in the fair, or that Amy had considered taking credit for it. Both of her sisters felt that Amy had learned her lesson well, and it was up to her to tell Marmee if she wished, when she was ready.

And Amy *would* tell Marmee, someday soon. But for now, she wanted to enjoy her sweet home, and her mother's return.

"No scrapes to speak of," Meg said.

"But we did make a new friend," Jo put in as she poked at the fire. "Adelaide .Montgomery is her name. She's Amy's age, and she's got her various faults—as we all do, mind you—but we've had her to tea twice, and we might give her a part in the next theatrical. We taught her how to faint, and she was capital. Much better than Amy, who just can't fall properly."

"She's barely better," Amy corrected. "And it's only because you didn't catch me that time, Jo. You've frightened me forever. I'm afraid I'll hit my head again."

"You fell on the sofa, you goose, so don't look for my sympathy," Jo said with a laugh.

"I can see that nothing has changed," Marmee said, her eyes twinkling.

"But something did happen," Beth broke in. "Amy won second prize in the art exhibition at the Winter Fair. Her prize was a box of new paints, and she's done new drawings of all of us."

Marmee laid her hand on the top of Amy's head. "That's wonderful, Amy. You must tell me all about it." She fingered the pink satin ribbon in Amy's golden hair. "And where did you get this pretty ribbon? You've been asking me for blue."

"I discovered something important while you were away, Marmee," Amy told her. She leaned against her mother's skirts, happy and content to be in her sweet home, surrounded by those who loved her best, no matter how few or many prizes she might win. "Pink is now my favorite color!"